My Baggage

By: December
Weestrand

To all who helped me stay motivated to finish this book. Special shout out to my family, Ms.De Lacey, my friends involved and 5 Seconds of Summer for inspiring me.

Table of Contents

"You've gotta let it go, you're losing all your hope
Nothing left to hold, locked out in the cold
Your painted memories then washed out all the scenes
I'm stuck in between a nightmare and lost dreams."

5 Seconds of Summer, Broken Home

Entry 1: Do I Have To?

I'm not ready for this. For everything. I am scared. I do not want to go back to reality. It is not very nice out there, I am not sure if I can handle it. I know that I need to go back eventually, I just did not think it would happen this soon is all. I guess I don't get much of a choice, do I? Oh well, here I go. Wish me luck. I am going to need it.

Entry 2: My Own Time

They are taking me off of my medication today. You see I am a pretty messed up person. I have no idea who is reading this. This is supposed to be my personal journal to document all of my feelings and thoughts to help me cope with things. Or so they all tell me. I know that if you are reading this right now, they all lied. They always lie to me.

Always.

I do not really want to write in this thing. They are not forcing me to. I just know that if I write in this, it will make them happy. I bet you may be wondering who "they" are. Well, "they" are my doctors, therapists and others of the like. People who think that writing in here about my feelings will help me to be happy. It will help me to cope.

I hate that word. Cope. Maybe I want to deal with things on my own. In my own way, the way I want. I do not want to "do it by the book", I do not want to do it the way all of the studies say will work. But oh well, I don't have much say in the matter.

I wanted to do this in my own time. Did you ever think of that? But they said that it was "time" to move on. How dare they say that? I know for a fact that they have never been through what I went through. So, how would they know it was "time", they don't. Nobody knows. Nobody but me.

I know they're going to read this when I fall asleep. But, maybe this really will help me. I'll just have to wait and see what happens.

Entry 3: Introductions

I know by now that you are most likely still wondering what happened to me that put me in this position. But I'll get to that later. For now I'll just tell you what I can about myself. They said to write like I was talking to another person, anyway and I haven't even introduced myself yet. How rude of me, I'm sorry. I mean, it seems like we are in for the long haul together. You may as well get to know me first before just listening (reading, you know what I mean) to me rant about things you do not know anything about. So just in case you do not know who I am already and you may have just found this journal by chance, I am going to tell you a bit about myself.

Hello, my name is Violet Lynn Andrews. I am

fifteen years old. I am naturally a quiet person but I can be loud and crazy when I want to. I do not really have a talent for much. Not that I know of anyway. I guess you could say that I am good at drawing. You could also say that I'm good at writing now too.

I still have no idea why they gave me a journal to write in and not a sketchbook or paints. I think they may be worried about my drawings. That is usually how I express myself. They must have thought that it wasn't helping and only making things worse. They don't understand me. I am more abstract and dark in my art at the moment due to my condition. They think it makes me more aggressive. I guess writing is supposed to be "healthier". But who really knows what is "healthier" or not.

Whoever is reading this, I do not know if you have ever seen me before and know what I look like. If not, then I am going to describe myself to help you visualize me better. I am quite a short person, I'm barely even 5 feet tall. I have naturally bright blonde hair that reaches the middle of my back. My eyes are somewhat of a purple/dark blue color or so I've been told. I know ironic isn't it? My name is Violet and my eyes look purple. Although I think that people just tell me my eyes look purple because of my name. I'm also not a really tan person either. But I think that is just because I don't see much sunlight anymore. I do not have many features that make me unique. I look somewhat average, maybe my hair is what makes me stand out, I'm not sure.

Entry 4: The Therapist

My therapist is weird. Her name is Miss Taylor. I'm not sure if you have met her before. Just in case you haven't I'll explain her. She is of average height with blue eyes and long brown hair that is always kept up in a bun. I think she should let her hair down more often, it might help her relax. You see, Miss Taylor can be bipolar. One day she is all nice and friendly and seems like a person I wouldn't mind talking to. But then another day she seems like every other adult and person in this building that doesn't and never will understand, she can be so uptight. It is almost like she's pregnant, but I know she doesn't have a boyfriend (I've asked before). Maybe that's what she needs.

Anyway, back to what I was going to say. My therapist, Miss Taylor, is weird. Today was one of the days that I had a session with her before my school class for the day. Miss Taylor has a tendency to wear too much makeup sometimes. I don't think she was very popular in school. I know that she is also a high school counselor aside from her job here. I can see her as a high school counselor wanting to help troubled kids. She probably has students she helps that went through the same things she did. I have also gathered that even though she has moved on and grown up, she still carries the insecurities she once had. She now just wants to help young people with problems like someone helped her once, or didn't help her. This is why I think I get along with her so much better than the other people here, she seems more real to me.

But I have no idea how Miss Taylor ended up working here. She is a high school counselor that also works as therapist for a mental hospital, with mostly teen patients. I don't know how she does it. I really would go insane or become totally depressed from hearing about other people's problems all day. I can barely talk about my own problems with someone else. Miss Taylor can be a strong person with other people's problems but not with her own.

Entry 5: Jayden

I just realized that I told you I was in a mental hospital in my last entry. I have no idea if you already knew where I was or not. But if you didn't, I am in a mental hospital. I didn't mean to end up in here. I didn't want to. It's all Jayden's fault, she is the one that ended up putting me here. Jayden Casey Kay is my best friend and has been since we were five years old. I know that she only did what she did out of love and worry for me. But it's all really unnecessary, I would have been fine.

Jayden is very short like me, under five feet in height, I am actually about an inch or so taller than her. She has dark brown eyes that almost look black at times and auburn red hair in a pixie cut. Jayden has a naturally pale complexion with a few freckles on her nose and cheeks.

She looks almost magical due to her small frame and complexion, her personality only adds to it. Jayden is a very loud and animated person, I am always reminding her of the volume of her voice. I still have no idea how we ended up being such good friends, with our personalities being such polar opposites. I guess we have some things in common but, if you met us separately, you would never think we were friends. Jayden is one of the only people that can bring out my "wild" side.

I miss her. But I am scared to talk to her after what happened. I'm not mad at her anymore for putting me here, I was at first. But, I've come to admit that she only did it because she cares. Maybe I'll write her a letter.

Entry 6: New Boy

Oh my god. Oh. My. God. Where have I been? He must be new. There is a guy sitting across the room from me and he keeps looking in my direction. He is not bad looking either. I know I sound like a total teenage girl interested in a guy she doesn't even know. So sue me, I don't care. He doesn't seem like the others here though. I'm one of the youngest people here. Most of everyone else is way older than me and the ones that are close to my age don't even look at me. Maybe he's been here for a while and I just haven't seen him. They made me leave my room today and be around other people since I tend to try to stay in my room as much as I can.

Oh, dear lord. Who is this boy and why does he keep looking at me? I'm nobody special.

Entry 7: Miss Taylor Knows All

Miss Taylor won't stop smiling at me.

I've been spending almost all of my time in the common room since I saw Mystery Guy. I'm calling him Mystery Guy until I can find out his name. I saw him once but he only passed through the room and down another hallway. I know he looked at me though.

I also know that Miss Taylor has noticed I haven't been in my room a lot lately. That or the nurses ratted me out. They are notorious for their gossip. She knows why too and now she won't stop smiling. Especially since I was trying to be sly and ask if we have gotten any new people closer to my age. She wouldn't tell me his name though, all she said was "Yes, yes we did". I know this is her way of trying to make me socialize. Which sucks, all I wanted was a name, but if I have to talk to him, I'll never know.

Entry 8: Insomniac

I have been up since 3 this morning. I couldn't sleep. I haven't been able to for the past few days. I can't hide from my memories anymore. They won't leave me alone. Why did they have to take me off of the medication completely? It's all finally gotten out of my system. Now I can't hold the dreams at bay anymore. I wish it wasn't like this. I don't have the energy to do anything anymore.

Why me? Why did it have to be me?

Entry 9: Better

Well I have begun to feel better. The dreams still come but I have been getting better at dealing with them. I hate my memories, I wish they would just go away. I bet I know what you are wondering. Yes, my memories and dreams are from that bad, bad thing that ultimately ended up putting me in the mental hospital. I-

What is that annoying noise? It has been bugging me for last 45 minutes. I thought that it would eventually go away but now it's getting on my nerves.

I can't handle it anymore, I need to go see what it is. I think it's coming from the room next to me. Great now it's getting louder. It sounds almost like music.

Entry 10: Him

Elliot. Elliot A Johnson. My Mystery Guy. His name is Elliot A Johnson. His middle name is just the letter A nothing else. It doesn't stand for anything and it is not short for anything either. He said that people always ask about it when he tells them his full name.

I know, I know I bet you are totally confused as to how I know this. I have implied that I have talked to him. That I have spoken words to him and he has spoken back. Yes, I have met him and talked to him. I don't know what it is about him that makes me like this. I have no idea why every time I think about him I get almost light headed and my stomach twists into knots. Okay, I know you are probably wanting to know some details as to how all of this went down, so here it is.

As you know, I heard some noise coming from the room next to mine and it was driving me nuts. So, I went over to see what in the world was making that noise. But, as I peeked in the doorway I saw *him*, he was sitting there at his desk on the computer. Music was playing through speakers on either side of the monitor. All of a sudden he looked up and noticed me in the doorway. I was so shocked that he was in the room next to me and that he was playing music.

You see, they took my music privileges away a while ago. All I am allowed to play now is classical music and I'm not into that at all. They told me that the music I was playing was upsetting some of the other patients. I wasn't exactly playing happy-go-lucky music, but still, they didn't have to take away *all* of the good music.

Anyway he had noticed me in the doorway and I wasn't ready to be social yet, especially with him. I turned around and leaned against the wall outside the door. My heart was beating a thousand miles a minute and I could feel that my eyes were as big as saucers. I couldn't have been more embarrassed, I mean he had caught me peeking in the doorway at him. But after a minute, nothing changed and he didn't come through the door and his music was still paying. I could make out some of the lyrics.

I want to breathe you in like you're vapor.
I want to be the one you remember.
I want to feel your love like the weather.
All over me, all over me

I recognized the song as Vapor by 5 Seconds of

Summer. 5 Seconds of Summer is one of my favorite bands along with nevershoutnever. Their lyrics really speak to me. So, me being me and not thinking, I peeked in the doorway again. He was looking right at the door, like he knew that I would look in again or that he didn't know if I was there for sure. He was looking right at me. I couldn't do it. I was a chicken, a coward. I leaned back against the wall outside the door again. I heard the music stop and his footsteps coming to the doorway. He then poked his head around the door like I had done and smiled at me. He told me how he had seen me around but didn't know my name. I was frozen in my spot and couldn't form any words. It was like my mouth had disconnected from my brain. All he did was smile at me.

His smile.

I think he could tell I was shy, he invited me in to talk. My feet seemed to have a mind of their own as they followed him into his room. He sat back in his desk chair as I perched on the edge of his bed. He told me his name and all I could think about was how it fit him perfectly. I still couldn't speak, my voice box seemed to have stopped working. I think he could tell that I hadn't really had a normal conversation in a while. He looked down suddenly at my lap and I noticed that I was playing with my fingers and hair, a habit I had when I was nervous.

But instead of just sitting there awkwardly, he continued to talk. He told me about how people always ask about his middle name and other random things. I wasn't really paying that close attention. I was too preoccupied with staring at him. I had never seen him up close before and his sheer beauty shocked me. He was tall and I mean tall, not just normal tall because everyone is taller than me since I'm so short. He had green eyes so deep that I could get lost in them forever. They were almost an emerald color. His hair was a deep brown that lay haphazardly on his head with a beanie placed loosely on top, but it looked good on him. I noticed that he was wearing jeans which was weird. Patients here rarely ever wore jeans. He also had on a black V-neck T-shirt.

He was looking at me weird. I hadn't realized why until he smiled and repeated his question. He has asked me what my name was. I could feel myself blushing. What was wrong with me? I mean come on! My voice seemed to be able to work finally as I quietly told him my name. All he did was smile slightly to himself and he said how it made sense. He said I looked like a Violet.

After that my voice seemed to be in overdrive, I just couldn't shut up. Did that boy ever stop smiling? I swear his face has to start to hurt eventually right? We ended up talking for almost 3 hours. Eventually I relaxed. I don't know what it is about that boy. He just makes me feel so strange and the way he would look at me, I've never had anyone look at me like that before. Unfortunately lights out came all too soon and I had to go back to my room.

I didn't have any nightmares that night. I woke up happy this morning and started writing this, I thought you may want to know what had happened last night with my strange noise.

Entry 11: Not Good Today

It has been a bad day. A very bad day. I guess that I have "been showing some unusual behavior". I don't why they just don't see that I have been acting different because for once I'm actually halfway happy. So now they are putting me on new medicine. I'm so mad about this, I can't even begin to describe it. All the garbage that they threw in my face as to why I now have new meds. Honestly it is like they don't want me to be happy.

To make this day worse, Elliot is gone. I have no idea where he is, but all I know is that I couldn't find him anywhere. I was hoping that I would be able to talk to him again. I was hoping that he would be able to make me feel better. That today wasn't a total waste.

Entry 12: Elliot Found

I found Elliot. He said he was sorry when I asked where he was and that I had been looking for him. They had taken him away for secluded therapy. I remember when I had to do that. He must've been here for a full month and a half since that's usually when they pull new patients for secluded therapy. That's when I realized that I had no idea as to why he was here.

I mean most of us know why we are here and a lot of the time it's the first question to be asked when you meet someone new. I almost asked him out of curiosity but I realized that I didn't want to tell him why I was here. I knew that if I asked him that I would be expected to tell him my story too. I'm just not ready for that yet. I'm almost surprised that he didn't ask me, but I'm not complaining.

Yeah, yeah I know your ears probably perked up there for second, since you don't know why I'm here either. Too bad, I'm not saying anything about it.

Anyway, I did ask him about himself. You know that basic questions, the favorites etc. His favorite color is green and his favorite food is anything Italian. He has 2 siblings, an older and younger sister, their names are Bailey and Alexis. I, in return, told him about my older brother, Stefan. I also told him about Jayden and he believes that I should write a letter to her too, so maybe I will. We talked until lights out again and I had to go back to my room. So here I sit, writing this to you by the dim moonlight coming from my window.

I know such a poetic line. Well I think it's about time I got some sleep, I'll write to you another time.

Entry 13: Cloudy

I don't feel like myself anymore. I feel like I want to cry and scream at the same time. I feel like a haze has dropped over my thoughts. I can't think clearly anymore. They have injected me with something and I don't feel like myself anymore. I can feel my personality slipping away by the minute. I hate this. I wish this wasn't happening to me. I don't know if I can keep this up much longer, it's becoming more difficult to write. Here they come. They're coming for me, I can see them coming down the hallway through my partly open door. I know that they are coming here to "help me relax". Everyone here knows that if they come to help you "relax" that they are coming into your room with a needle and guards. They are going to make me sleep. I'm not sure what I've done to deserve this. I know that

I did something, but I can't remember what it was anymore, thanks to this medicine they injected me with. I can feel my emotions dissolving away. I guess whatever I did, it was bad enough for them to decide that just making me dazed is not enough. That I need to sleep for as long as they want me to be asleep. Here they come. Wish me luck.

Entry 14: Gossip

I am finally awake. I still can't feel much though, they're keeping me numb. I have been out for roughly 36 hours. I don't know how long they are going to keep me this way. It makes it harder to write to you, having my feelings blocked like this.

I had a visitor today. Elliot dropped by to see how I was doing. He told me that I'm the talk of the ward. Whatever I did was big enough that everyone is talking about it. I have never done anything big enough to become gossip before. I almost do not want to know what I did. I think he noticed my inability to respond and realized they had me on some serious meds. He talked for a little bit longer and seemed to gauge what my reactions might have been, based on the look in my eyes. Then he smiled at me and said his goodbyes, patting me on the hand before walking out of the door.

I really wish I was not on this medicine. I just had an opportunity to talk to Elliot again and I lost it. They took it away from me. I think I might have felt a little sadder about it if I could feel anything at all. I can *almost* miss him.

Entry 15: News

I can finally feel again. I'm not sure if I'm entirely pleased about that. The whole thing that happened with Elliot has left me feeling embarrassed. I don't like people seeing me when I'm on those meds and he probably saw what I did to get put on those meds.

I can now remember what I did that was so bad. I was with Miss Taylor during one of our regular sessions. She wanted to talk about it, the terrible thing that happened to me. I should have seen this coming to be honest, it's been so long since I last talked about it and even then I didn't say much. I was using my usual tactics to get around talking about it, but she just kept pressing me. She just wouldn't let me be. Most of the time she gives up after a while but this time was different. This time she wouldn't give up. I couldn't take it anymore. I just couldn't talk about it, not now when things were kind of looking up for me. I sort of may have flipped out on her and went into a rampage. I can't quite remember exactly what I did, but it was still pretty bad. I understand why they knocked me out now. They're putting me on new meds again to help control my "temper". I also have more therapy sessions each week and I have to go to secluded therapy for a week, starting tomorrow. So that means I won't be able to write for a week. Wish me luck.

Entry 16: Back Again

Well I'm finally back from secluded therapy. It wasn't that bad since I kind of knew what to expect from my first time being there. It was almost peaceful actually, without having to be worried about many social interactions. At least I didn't have to face anyone that saw my outburst for a week. Which here, is just enough time for everyone to forget about it if they don't see you to remind them. That's all I got for now, nothing to really note on. I haven't seen Elliot again since the day he visited me. Hopefully he doesn't think that I'm a total loon now. Ironic since we are both in a mental hospital.

Entry 17: My New Leaf

Okay, so I'm trying to turn over a new leaf. I want to fix things with Jayden. I think that I've fully forgiven her for putting me here and I want her to know that I'm not mad anymore. Well since I can't just send her brain waves to come and visit me and I can't call her since I don't have a phone. Also, even though I have internet access, I'm restricted from all social media and can't message her that way. I have officially gone completely old school and I wrote her a letter. Here I'll leave you a copy of my letter. I know it's not very long but I didn't really know what to say.

Dear Jayden,

I know that we haven't spoken in a long time. I just

wanted to let you know that I miss you. I'm not mad at you anymore like I was. I guess that I haven't been mad for a while now, I've just been hesitant to talk to you. But I really miss you and I'm trying to turn over a leaf I guess. I know that you only did what you did out of love and I can see where you were coming from. So much has been happening here lately.

I had a meltdown about not wanting to talk about it and got myself knocked out, drugged and sent to secluded therapy. All in all I guess it wasn't that bad.

But here is the big thing. There's a boy. A really cute and nice boy. His name is Elliot and he's 17 years old. He has been nothing but nice to me even throughout my whole emotional roller-coaster. I would love it if you could meet him. Maybe you could come visit.

How is everyone? How are you? What have you been up to lately, any new adventures? Any new love interests? I haven't talked to you in forever, let me know what's going on. Remember I don't have a phone or access to social media, so you'll have to either write me back or visit. Please contact me back. I miss you.

Forever and always your BFF and sister,
Violet Lynn Andrews
P.S. I found my pen as you can see. Remember all the times we would pass notes in class? This brings back some old memories.

I have mailed out her letter. I hope she contacts me back, I miss her a lot and it would be nice to hear from her again. She used to try to write to me before when I was first sent here, trying to get me to talk to her. But eventually she gave up and told me that she would give me my space and wait for me to contact her. I hope she still feels the same way. It took me forever to find my pens. Once Jayden and I were at the store and we found these purple and blue pens, our two favorite colors. We would always pass notes to each other in class or we would just write each other little notes randomly. She was always the blue pen and I was always the purple pen.

Entry 18: No Reply, From Anyone

I haven't heard back from Jayden yet. I guess I shouldn't be so impatient. I mean I did have to contact her through the snail mail. I wonder if she has even gotten my letter yet. I miss her so much. I need my best friend. Why did I push her away for so long? I guess I brought it on myself if she doesn't want to talk to me anymore.

I still haven't talked to Elliot since before I left for secluded therapy. I hope he isn't avoiding me. I did see him though, I just wasn't able to talk to him. He was walking through the common room but he didn't seem to notice that I was sitting there. I don't know.

Entry 19: Letters

I got a letter today. It was from Jayden. I was so relieved when it was delivered to my room. I was worried for a while, I didn't know if she would answer me back or not. I feel so much better. Here I'll put it in here for you to read.

Hey Vi,

What's up with all of the formality? I mean come on! I'm your best friend, you don't need to be so formal about everything. Everyone else is doing pretty fine or so I've heard. I haven't had the chance to talk to any of them in a while.

I miss you too. I was so happy when I got your letter that I actually cried and then I screamed in excitement before I even opened the envelope. My roommate gave me the evil eye, she wasn't very happy with me anyway. I guess I'm too joyful for her.

You see, I'm at a camp. Yeah, I know me at a camp, totally unexpected. I didn't really want to go but mom and dad forced me to. I mean who forces their teenage daughter to go to a camp for the first time. I guess its okay but I would much rather be with you. My roommate is kind of distant and mean. She never wants to do anything together, I think she hates me. She may just be mad at me 'cause she wanted to bunk with her friends that she always bunks with and hangs out with at camp. But instead she got stuck with me and was forced to give me a tour and explain things to me since it is my first year here. (She didn't really show me anything, I still keep getting lost).

But I did find someone nice and they helped me out. We hang out together with her friends. Her name is Emilie and she's really nice. But we aren't that close, I don't feel like I can tell her everything like

I can tell you.

So... this Elliot character. What's up with that? Are you 2 an item yet? I bet you are. Who could not love you, with all your charm and everything? You're a catch. I would LOVE to meet him. I think I like him already for not judging you about anything. But if he hurts you then I'm going to have to hurt his face. Does he know about, you know **it**?

I'm sorry for what happened. That was totally unfair of them. All because you were not ready to talk about your past yet. They should have respected how you felt, and when you started to get worked up over it, they should have backed off and given you some space. Not just push you harder and make everything worse than it already was.

I would totally visit you. If I could. But unfortunately I am stuck here at this camp. I mean it's not even a special camp for anything, not like an arts camp or something. I don't even know how my parents got the idea to send me here. It is just camp. That's it nothing else. I miss you loads though! Write me back, love you! Also

I totally remember that you don't have any access to a phone or any social media.

Your loving BFF and sis,
Jayden
P.S. You can just write me back at the camp address until I get back home. That way I can get your letters back faster and I don't have to wait for my parents to forward it to me. I found my pen too. I'm glad we can do this again. It really does feel like the old days when we would pass notes in class.

This letter has made my day. I feel so much better about everything and I do plan on writing her back soon. I was worried for nothing, we are still as close as we were before all of this happened.

Entry 20: Flowers

I talked to Elliot today. I was sitting in the common room and he came up to me wanting to talk. He told me that there was something he wanted to show me. So I followed him outside and he led me toward the gardens, which is one of my favorite places to hide out here. The whole time I was following him I kept wondering what it was he wanted to show me and why it was outside. He took me through all the gardens and to a small private garden room that patients were not allowed to be in. So naturally I stopped and told him we weren't supposed to go in there. But all he did was shake his head, smile and tell me that it was fine, we had special permission. I was still a little hesitant about it, but eventually I went in with him.

I was so surprised at what was in there when we

walked in. The room was not very big. But it was full of all different kinds' roses and lilies along with a few other species flowers that complimented them nicely to make them stand out more. My two favorite flowers that were almost never in the main gardens, roses and lilies. There was also a small sitting area with a table and plush chairs. I just stood there in awe, taking it all in. How did Elliot know that roses and lilies were my favorite flowers? Most people just assume that my favorite flowers are violets. Why did he do this and bring me here? I mean we have not talked very often and it's not like we were a couple or anything.

I turned to him in shock to ask him about it but he beat me to it. He told me that he remembered what my favorite flowers were from one of our previous conversations. I had forgotten that I'd even told him. He also told me that it seemed like I was going through some things and maybe I needed a pick-me-up. I was extremely touched that he'd even noticed. Elliot also said that I didn't need to tell him about what was bothering me unless I wanted to. He must've also noticed my hesitation when anything about my past was brought up. He just wanted me to have a place to escape to if I needed it and that was all mine, totally secluded. This was the reason why he has been so distant lately. He wanted to be able to have it ready in time to surprise me. We were also the only patients allowed to be in here. It was completely ours.

I was stunned that anyone would do something like this for me. We sat in the garden for a while before going in together for dinner. Today has been such a good day because of this, I feel really touched that he thought of me. I still don't know how he pulled it off, but it doesn't matter now, it only matters that he did it.

Entry 21: The Terrible Thing

Well I finally did it. I talked about it. I talked about my past and what happened to me that put me here. I felt like it was time and I was so peaceful after the events from earlier this week. I couldn't put it off any longer and I knew that I would have to do it eventually. Better late than never, I guess and to do it while I was still in a relatively calm mood. I don't really know when I decided that I would talk about it. Miss Taylor didn't even bring it up, I just started to talk about it. I almost can't believe that I talked about it after all this time, I didn't think I could. I think that it was easier for me to do it this way, I had somewhat of an inner peace while I was talking. I'm kind of relieved that I've finally gotten it off of my chest. I'm sure you want to hear about it too. So here it is, this is the terrible thing that happened to me and left me broken.

I was 14 when it happened. It's been just over a full year since it happened. I almost can't believe that it's been that long. It was the worst day of my life and always will be.

Everything started out fine it was a perfectly normal day. A nice spring day and I remember that it was warmer than usual and it just seemed like it would be a really good day. I was so completely wrong though, it was nowhere near a good day. I went to school and it was a Friday. The day breezed by, the teachers along with the students all seemed to have spring fever and were ready for the weekend. We didn't end up doing much work that day. My friends and I had plans for Saturday, we were going to go to the next town over. But now I can't remember what we were going to do once we got there. I went home at the end of the school day and everything seemed normal, everyone doing their own thing. My dad was finishing up some work and mom was busy in the kitchen. Stefan, my older brother, was in his room playing video games like he always did. Nothing seemed out of the ordinary. After dinner we all decided to rent a movie and was even able to get Stefan to watch it with us, which was rare he usually didn't spend much time outside of his room. After the movie we all went back to our own things, Stefan to his room and me to mine. I'm sure what my parents were doing though.

It was later when it happened. 11:16 to be exact. I don't know why I remember that so clearly. There was a loud crash from downstairs and my parents shouting. I thought one of them had just knocked something over and was upset about it. That was until I heard a third voice. That's when I got worried. I went over to Stefan's room to see if he knew what was going on. He just looked at me weird and shrugged. We weren't that close. But we both decided to go down and see what was going on. What happened once we got downstairs changed our lives forever. There was no going back.

Both of our parents were being held at gunpoint by two different men in clown masks. I know how original, clown masks. There was another man standing there with a gun of his own in a red sweatshirt and he seemed to be the leader. I remember in this exact moment, asking myself if it was all real. Red, the leader, started yelling at my parents, saying that they shouldn't have lied about there being others in the house. My parents cringed and looked at us with pleading eyes. But I don't know what they were pleading about, or were they apologizing for what they thought was to come. Red then turned toward my brother and me and told us to get on our knees with our hands behind our heads across from our parents. I couldn't move, I was in too much shock. Stefan grabbed my arm and gently pulled me as he got down, giving me a look that told me that I needed to do as they said. He snapped me out of my reverie and I got down across from my dad. I stared into his eyes and the fear I saw in them scared me more than anything and would haunt me forever. My dad had always been strong and brave and to see him that scared made me even more afraid.

We were told that if any of us resisted, talked out of turn or moved, one of us would be shot immediately. I stayed perfectly silent and still as they began to pat down my brother and I, looking for any weapons. The clown patting me down seemed a little too happy to be doing it and his hands wandered. I bit my lip to stop myself from crying. They took our phones and put them somewhere else in the room. I noticed that one of the other clowns had a scar on his neck and the third had a burn mark on his forearm. Scar kept a gun pointed at my brother and I as Burn kept his on my parents. Red told my mother to get up, she rose hesitantly. But when he told her to go the bedroom, my father opened his mouth and began to protest and his protests soon died when a gun was trained directly to the center of my mom's forehead. She shuffled sadly to the bedroom and Red told Burn to go with her. Scar started to whine but was shut up with a look from Red. I could only imagine what was happening to her. Soon my father was forced to go back there too and Stefan and I were left alone with Red. He kept looking at me. We didn't dare do anything.

My parents came back awhile later and we were all forced to go and sit on the couch. I sat next to my dad and brother. My mom was crying silently and dad had a haunted look on his face. I could tell that he wanted to comfort my mom but he couldn't otherwise one of us would die. Scar put his gun to my forehead and told me to stand up and sit on the loveseat next to the couch. Scar sat on one side of me with Red on the other, Red put his hand on my knee and slowly slid it up. I looked at my family trying not to focus on it. A single, silent tear streamed down my face. Something seemed to snap in my brother and he stood and went to make a move like he was going to move Red and Scar away from me. But he was soon stopped when Burn shot mom in the chest. Stefan sat back down in shock and none of us moved. My dad finally snapped out of it and caught her as she started to fall over. He held her as she bled out. "I warned you." said Red.

Mom suddenly started coughing and we all knew she wasn't going to last long. I sobbed silently as she took her last breath. Red made me get up and sit back in my previous spot on the couch. Then Burn and Scar took my mother from my dad and dragged her into the other room. My dad couldn't take it and he lashed out, going straight toward Burn. He was almost immediately shot in the chest, right over his heart. I collapsed on my knees to catch him and I held him as I watched the light leave his eyes. Right before he took his last breath he mouthed "I love you." I ran my hand over his eyes to close them as Burn and Scar took him to the other room to join my mom. "Either one of you want to try anything?" Red asked us. We both shook our heads, holding on to each other.

I was soon told to go to the bedroom. I knew what was coming next, and gave Stefan's hand one last squeeze as I got up. Once I made it to the bedroom, I was told to sit and wait on the bed. Stefan and Burn, who had stayed behind, soon entered the room. You can guess what happened next. I was raped by both Red and Scar with my brother as a witness. They sat us both back on the couch and my brother wouldn't sit anywhere near me, I think he was scared to get close to me, he knows that not is not a good time to be physically close, even if it was accidental. I was terrified of what would happen next.

Until my phone started ringing. Red looked at me and then pulled it out if his pocket and told me to answer it but not to try anything. It was Jayden. I answered it as calmly as I could as Red held his gun to my head. She chatted normally and Red made me put her on speaker. She then got suspicious of how quiet I was being. Red gave me a look that told me to fix it. I told her that everything was fine and that I was just working on my blog so I was distracted. She knows I don't have a blog but it was a thing we had come up with if either of us got in trouble and needed help. She asked what chapter I made it to and I told her 11, which was code for her to call 911. She caught on and told me that she'd call back in an hour and she couldn't wait to read what happened.

I was relieved when she hung up. Red took my phone back and lucky for me none of them suspected anything and Stefan was smart enough to play along since he knew about our "blog" plan. Scar walked into the other room and came back with rope in his hand. Red ordered us both to the walk into the pantry in the kitchen. We were then tied with our backs to each other. They proceeded to put tape over our mouths as well. With a stroke to my cheek from Red all three of them left the pantry. I sat in silence with Stefan as we both awaited what was coming next. We heard a lot of banging around for a while and some shouts. Then we heard what sounded like a door slamming and complete silence. We sat there for about an hour and a half until the pantry door finally opened. In came the police and behind them was Jayden.

The clowns still haven't been found. So now you know what happened to me. That ultimately caused me to end up here in the hospital. I ended up snapping at Jayden on accident and that caused her to question my sanity. She went to Stefan who is now my legal guardian since he was already 18 when it happened. He agreed with her and didn't really know what to do with me so they sent me here. Stefan is currently studying abroad somewhere in Europe. I haven't heard from him since I've been taken here. I think that he's scared to see me since what happened. He didn't really know how to help me after everything. He was having a hard enough time dealing with it himself. We were never that close anyway and I understand why he left and never really tried to be there. It's weird but I understand.

So there it is, that's everything. Hopefully I haven't scared you off or anything and I don't want your pity. That's the main thing. I know what happened to my family and me. The last thing I need is for you to feel sorry for me. It never helps, all it does is bring up all of the sadness and fear I felt. You wouldn't be helping me move on.

I shocked Miss Taylor into complete silence. She couldn't form a single word. I was never able to talk to the police either. Stefan couldn't either, as soon as we were found he just acted as if nothing happened. I think he was scared to admit to himself that it even happened. As a result the police report was never finished since they couldn't get eyewitness evidence. They went as far as they could with what they had. The report would be finished now. Miss Taylor is required to record all of our sessions.

I feel as if a weight has been lifted off of me. But all of the feelings from that night have come back. I miss my parents and even my brother. I don't know if I can tell Jayden about it or Elliot for that matter. Maybe I can get my hands on a copy of the recording so I wouldn't have to do any of the talking. This is as far as I can go for now. Hopefully it's enough.

Entry 22: Progress

My Internet restrictions have been lifted since I've shown "significant progress". The first thing I did was email Jayden since she mentioned in a postcard to me the other day that she now has her phone with internet access back and that it's the only thing that's keeping her sane. She replied within an hour of me sending it. She is *very* happy that I have my internet back and asked what I did to earn it. I told her and she didn't press me for details since it's a sensitive subject. Jayden said that she was getting 2 weeks off from camp and that she is going to come and visit me first thing. I can't wait it's been forever since I last seen her. She also wants to meet Elliot. I have yet to inform him of this, but I will soon. Wish me luck, I'll update later.

Entry 23: Approved

I talked to Miss Taylor and she has approved of Jayden coming to visit me. I can't wait for her to come. She's coming next week on her break from camp. I'm actually scared to see her. It's been so long and she could be a totally different person by now. What if I don't recognize her? What if she doesn't recognize me? What if we can't be like we were before everything that happened? What if her and Elliot don't get along? What if Elliot doesn't want to meet her? I still haven't talked to him about it yet. I've been putting it off. What if... I could go on for days playing the "what if" game.

Entry 24: Telling Elliot

So I talked to Elliot and he barely even flinched. I mean I tried to tell him how hard Jayden can be on people. He almost seems excited for her to come. I'm probably just overreacting and there's nothing I should be worried about. She comes in exactly one week from today. I can't decide if I'm really ready for this, too late now. Hopefully all goes good. Miss Taylor has been down my throat since she found out about Jayden's upcoming visit. She keeps telling me about all of the progress that I've made. I also told Elliot about what happened to me. He took it all very well, better than I thought he would. He was extremely supportive and said that he was very touched that I was comfortable with him enough to tell him. Well it's time for dinner, I have to go, and I'll write more later when I have a chance. Bye.

Entry 25: Soon

Jayden comes tomorrow. It's exactly 11:46 and Jayden is coming first thing in the morning. Maybe I'm not ready anymore. I'm way too nervous for this. I can't sleep at all, maybe I jumped the gun on this and didn't think everything through enough. It's been so long since I last saw Jayden. What if things are too different between us now? I can hear them coming, the nurses are about to tell me that I need to turn my light off and go to bed. I'll let you know what happens tomorrow when I get a chance.

Entry 26: The Visit

So Jayden just left. She stayed here from the beginning to the end of visiting hours. She and Elliot seemed to get along well. I'll have to ask Jayden what she thought of him next time I talk to her. She told me she won't be able to come back tomorrow because her parents want to do some family barbecue thing, but she told me to call her tomorrow after my lunch to talk. I wish I knew what she thought of Elliot. I wish I knew how I thought of him. I wonder how he ended up here in the first place. But who am I to talk? I'm sure he wonders the same about me and I don't want to talk about my past, so I won't push him on his.

Sometimes I wish we had met under different circumstances at a different time and place. But at the same time it's the best thing that we met here and now. He's given me hope I think, he's shown me that maybe I can move on with my life and forgive myself and others. I still blame myself for my parents' death and Stefan's suffering. That maybe if I was smarter I would've been able to save my parents and prevent Stefan from having to worry. Jayden would've been better off too, not having to be bothered by a broken best friend. But at the same time I know that these things are meant to happen in a way. We are supposed to experience these things to grow. Some things are worse than others but maybe it was destined to happen, that it needed to happen to us. That way we can become the people we are meant to be.

Yeah I know, I sound like one of those people that are always talking about the philosophical meaning of life. Sometimes, we just need that kind of explanation to make us feel better. That everything happens for the greater good of things and it's all meant to be.

I'm glad Jayden came today and I'm glad she's my friend. I'm truly lucky to have her.

Entry 27: Jayden's Suffering

Jayden is dying, according to her. The family barbeque that she had to go to today is horrid, she said that all her family wants to talk about is her life decisions and her plans for the future. Jayden isn't so sure about what she wants to do yet, she wants to try everything she can before she settles with one option and it bothers her when people keep asking her about it, when her answer is always the same.

We spent most of our phone call talking about funny memories with her relatives and her ranting about how boring the barbeque was, until her dad made her hang up and socialize more. I never got the nerve to bring up Elliot though. I'd have to ask her about it next time.

Come to think of it, I haven't seen Elliot all day. I

wonder where he's at, it's probably nothing.

Entry 28: Adventure

Jayden got permission for me to leave the hospital with her for a few hours. So she just had to take me shopping of course. I was so happy when she told me, it feels like it's been an eternity since I've really been outside. It was nice, we got some new clothes and lotions.

It was nice to be able to be with Jayden in a normal setting again and hang out. It was just like old times and it gave me a sort of inner peace.

Jayden had some things to do today at home so she left after dropping me off back at the hospital. The freedom was nice while it lasted. I still haven't seen Elliot anywhere and every time I try to ask one of nurses about him, they act like they didn't hear me.

Something must have happened and it's got to be bad.

If no one will talk about it, then it's something serious. I hope he's okay.

Entry 29: Confusion

Jayden has come by to see me almost every day for the 2 weeks she had off of camp. Today was her last day before she had to go back. She's not exactly *happy* about it, but I told her we could still email until she came back for good. She asked about Elliot a few times, but I think she picked up that I didn't want to talk about it. I still have yet to see him since the last time I wrote.

I'm starting to worry about him. I've tried asking the nurses and Miss Taylor about it and no one will answer my questions. What could be so bad that no one would talk about it?

....

I heard Miss Taylor talking to my Doctor about me. It seemed like they were trying to decide if they should tell me something. "I think she's in the right state of mind to tell her without causing any harm." said Miss Taylor.

Maybe it was about Elliott, but that only made me more nervous for what it could be. What could have happened to Elliot that I had to be in the right state of mind so the information wouldn't cause any harm?

Entry 30: Elliot's Condition

I'm not sure what to think. Miss Taylor has just informed me that Elliot was in the hospital. She wouldn't go into much detail about it because she said it wasn't her place. I understand that but it only makes me more worried. She said he was recovering well from an accident that happened about 2 weeks ago. The last time I had seen him was 2 weeks ago. She told me that he'd been in a medically induced coma to help him recover, that's why it had been so long since I'd heard anything. Miss Taylor said that I was one of the first things he asked about when he woke up.

I was touched that he had thought of me, I've been so worried about him. Although now I'm still worried. What kind of accident had he been in? What had happened that caused him to need to be put a coma? I didn't press Miss Taylor for details, for which I think she was grateful. I k new it wasn't her place and I wasn't going to make this harder on her than it already was.

I don't know what to think. Hopefully I'll get to visit him soon. I wonder if he's in this hospital, just in a different ward. I'll have to ask Miss Taylor about it.

....

I just got off of the phone with Jayden. She seems concerned about Elliot, but she told me not to overreact. Jayden reassured me that things would turn out okay since he was awake now and just had to finish healing before he would be back to normal. Although, she does seem just as worried as me as to what had happened that put him in that position. I just hope everything turns out okay.

Entry 31: Surprise

I'm still in shock from what happened yesterday. I have not been able to see Miss Taylor today to ask her if I can visit him. I hope she's not avoiding me. Oh, here she comes now!

....

Miss Taylor said she was looking for me. I guess Elliot has refused to answer any questions or cooperate with any of the doctors or nurses until he saw me. But visiting hours are over in 15 minutes so I have to go first thing tomorrow. I'm so nervous, I wonder why he has to see me before he will do anything. Wish me luck, I'm going to need it.

Entry 32: Elliot's Story

So I just got back from visiting Elliot. He looked bad, but on the road to recovery. I could tell that he was trying to put on a brave face. Although he did seem really relieved when I walked in. His face and knuckles were bruised and his right hand was wrapped like he had sprained it. He made me give him a hug even though I was afraid of hurting him.

I didn't ask what happened but he told me anyway.

He got permission to go and visit his little sister, Alexis, while she was in town. He said that she had been dating this guy for a while and now and Elliot didn't like him. But Elliot didn't like him because he was always rude and seemed like he was mentally abusive to her. She always denied it though whenever Elliot brought it up. But this time when Elliot saw her there were bruises on her arms. Elliot knew that it was her boyfriend so he went after him. They got in a fight and that was how he ended up in the hospital. Alexis' boyfriend had cheated in the fight and hit Elliot over the head with a baseball bat. The doctors said he was recovering well though.

Elliot also told me about how he had ended up in the mental hospital in the first place. I tried to tell him that he didn't need to but he insisted on it, saying was only fair since I had told him my story.

After Alexis was born, Elliot's father started drinking more often. He also started to get more violent with his mom and older sister by the time Elliot was 11, Alexis was 9 and Bailey was 13. He began to defend his mom and sister and thus causing him to be hurt instead. He was abused by his father both mentally and physically until he was 14 years old. That was the reason why he ended up in the mental hospital with me, it was because of all the trauma. When he seen that his sister was being hurt, it hit a nerve and caused him to go after the guy.

I stayed with Elliot for the rest of the day talking about nothing and everything at the same time. He said that he should be back up to the ward by the end of the week. I don't judge him for what happened when he was little, just like he didn't judge me for what happened to me. We both have a past and we're both a little messed up, but that's okay.

Entry 33: Stefan

I went back down to visit Elliot again today. He was looking a lot better. I stayed down there until lunch time when his mom came in. There was some awkward introductions before I left to give them some privacy and go to my session with Miss Taylor.

Miss Taylor said that I had been making significant progress lately and that there is a possibility that I could go home in the next few months. I'm not sure how I feel about that, there isn't really a home for me to go to though. I mean Stefan was somewhere in Europe last I heard and Jayden and I have only just begun to mend our relationship. Plus I would have to leave Elliot and I don't want to do that. We understand what it means to be here and I don't want to have to face the world alone. How could

I leave Elliot after he had shared his story, I wanted to be there for him, the way he has been there for me. I haven't told anyone about it yet. I'm going to wait until they actually decide to release me.

....

So something strange has happened. I got an email from Stefan of all people. That was something I was definitely not expecting. I had wondered if Jayden had been in contact with him and mentioned that I was doing better. But when I asked her she said she hadn't talked to him since he left for Europe, only the occasional postcard she would get from him to let her know that he was alright. I'll leave a print out of his email here.

Dear Violet,

I know that it's been such a long time since the last we talked. I'm sorry that I haven't been in touch. I know that it's not easy for you either after everything that happened. I shouldn't have left without much contact. I hope you can forgive me for everything.

I'm coming back to the US in a few weeks. I hope that I can visit you so we can talk. I know that I can't undo what I've done but I can try to make it up to you. I hope you'll give me a chance.

Sincerely,

Stefan

I'm not really sure what to make of all of this. It's

been forever since I've actually talked to Stefan. We weren't even that close before everything but after it became more difficult. Well its lights out and they're telling me I have to go to bed.

Entry 34: Response

I emailed Stefan back and said that I would like to talk to him when he gets back and that I'm open to trying again. He hasn't responded, so I don't think he got it yet.

I talked to Elliot about it today. He thinks it's a good thing and maybe this is an opportunity to help Stefan and me to make amends. Jayden feels the same way. I'm still not sure about it. This all just seems too strange to me, it's been so long since I've talked to Stefan. It makes me think that something has happened, causing him to reach out to me.

....

Stefan replied back and told me what day he was coming back. He also said that he would come and visit me as soon as he got back. I guess this is really happening.

Wish me luck.

Entry 35: Update

Well not much has happened in the past week. Elliot came back up to the ward although he is still healing a bit and can't do certain activities yet. I've talked to Jayden and she said camp was still hell but she was working on trying to get her parents to let her leave early. She thinks that she almost has them convinced and the fact that I'm doing better is helping her make a better case, she wants to visit me again. She's hoping that will guilt trip her parents to let her leave.

Stefan will be here in two days and I'm really nervous. I hope that everything goes okay while he's here. Wish me luck, I'm going to need it.

Entry 36: Update 2

Stefan will be here tomorrow. I know I should be happy but I'm just not so sure. Everyone keeps telling me that this a good thing and I should just relax about it. That everything will turn okay. I don't know why but I have a bad feeling about this. I just feel like something is wrong, but I can't tell what it is. I can barely sleep, I'm that worried, I'm not necessarily nervous anymore I'm just worried for what is to come.

Entry 37: I'M NOT OKAY

I was right. Things are not okay. Not at all okay. I don't know what to do anymore. I knew something was coming but not *this*. I didn't think it would ever happen, it never crossed my mind that it was a possibility. Why me? Why did it have to be me? What did I do to deserve all of this? Why couldn't things go right for once? Why couldn't I have just actually had a real opportunity to mend the bond between Stefan and me?

Stefan came to warn me, he didn't come to help fix our relationship, far from it. He received a letter. So did I but all of my mail is monitored. They are from the clowns. The ones from the accident that were never found. They sent us letters. I don't even know how they knew where we were. Stefan was in Europe traveling a lot and I've been in the hospital, they shouldn't have been able to find us. Nobody will let me read the letters, so I have no idea what they say. Stefan just kept saying that it didn't matter, it was just nonsense. But if it was just nonsense then he wouldn't come all the way back here to tell me about it. He could've just kept it a secret from me. But they still won't let me read them. The only thing I know is that the clowns just said some threats and other stuff. Everyone keeps telling me that the threats are all empty. They say that they don't want me to worry. But if they didn't want me to worry, then why are they even telling me all of this? When I asked them that they said that they thought I should know about them and to know it was under control.

Obviously it's not under control. They had Stefan come back just to tell me in person because they thought it would lessen the blow if it came from someone that was there with me and since he was the only one it had to be him. They also thought it should be face to face.

Things were just getting better too. I was finally kind of happy and now this happened.

I'm **not** okay.

Entry 38: Lost

I don't know what to do. They've found us, they know where we are. They could come for us. I already know that they hate me. I'm the reason they almost got caught. If they were going to get revenge on someone it would be me. They're going to come after me.

Everyone keeps telling me that I'm perfectly safe but I know that I'm not. I'm so close to leaving the hospital anyway. I don't want this to ruin my chances of getting out. But what about Elliot? We've gotten really close in the time we've known each other. What happens if I leave? I think that we are more than friends and I don't want to leave him behind.

I don't know how much time Elliot has left in the hospital. If he was close, it may take longer now due to the incident that happened. They may not think that he's stable enough now to leave. I can't leave him, I want to be able to help him and it'll be too difficult if I leave. I'd only see him during visiting hours.

But at the same time if I was able to leave then I don't know if I could keep coming back here. I mean there are so many memories and it could be too difficult to move on and build a life if I keep coming back. Either way I lose something.

The clowns are another issue. If I leave then I am in even more danger from them. They would have more opportunities to come after me. What about Stefan? They could still easily go after him. Then there's Jayden. Would they go after her to get back at me? If they can't get to me they could go for her. She is the one that called the cops and unintentionally ended up leading up to them almost getting caught. She just called me at the right time for me, wrong time for the clowns.

I don't know what to do. Things were going so well and now everything has gone downhill. It's overwhelming me, everything is happening all at once and it's too fast.

....

I just realized something. I haven't seen Stefan since he came in 2 days ago. I've checked and triple checked my email and he hasn't emailed me either. He left yesterday after only being here for 15 minutes. Did he leave again? Did he only come here to tell me that the clowns made contact? Did he even come here of his will? Did they make him come here because they thought it would be better to hear it from him? I wish we were closer, he's the only one that truly understands what happened that night.

Entry 39: More News

I have more news. Elliot just told me that his doctor is going to release him in three weeks. I'm happy for him but at the same time I know that I'll miss him. I could tell that he was glad to be leaving but knew that I wouldn't be going with him. We've gotten really close while we've been here and I think we're both afraid to leave each other. I think that I may even love him. But I don't know. We're close and I'm scared to be close to anyone. What if something happened and he got hurt? I don't really know what to do. I'll be all alone once he leaves. I don't want to be alone.

Entry 40: Opportunity

I have more news. So today was one of the days that I meet with both Miss Taylor and my doctor. I've been given a choice. They've talked with both Stefan and Jayden and have decided to leave decision up to me. They both think that I've made enough progress to be released in 3 weeks or I can stay for a few more months until the threats from the clowns are gone. If I leave now then I'll have to go to checkups often and have to go into some type of witness protection program to make sure I am safe from the clowns. But if I stay here then I don't know how long it'll be until I'll be able to leave.

I thought this would be an easy and quick decision. I thought I was ready to leave. I mean I didn't even want to come here. But now I don't know anymore. I've been here for over a year now. So much must've changed in the time I've been out of touch. There's also Elliot, if I leave we will only have a week apart between the times we leave. But even then, would we be able to see each other once I got out? They did say I had to go into a witness protection program.

Would things even be the same between us? We've only known each other in the hospital. What if things are too different between us? Would I stay with Stefan or Jayden? Or would it be too dangerous and put them at risk? Would anything in my life ever been normal again?

I told Miss Taylor and my doctor that I had to think about it. I called Jayden and talked to her about it. She said she got back into town the other day. She was going to come and visit but she got caught up in some family stuff. She heard about the clowns just a little while before I called her. She's not sure about what I should do either. She says to follow my heart and things could work out with Elliot if it was meant to be. I'll never know if I don't try first. I'm not sure what to do. It seems like I'm sure of anything these days.

Entry 41: Decision

So I've thought about it and I've come to a conclusion. I'm going to leave the hospital. I've talked to Miss Taylor and she said a detective has been assigned to my case will come in the next few days to talk about my safety. I haven't told anyone else yet about what I've decided.

....

I emailed Jayden the news and she seemed happy, already planning things for us to do together. I also told Elliot and he seemed really happy about it. He understood all of my worries and doesn't seem to think much would change between us, I hope he's right.

I haven't been able to get ahold of Stefan yet. I know I shouldn't worry, but what if something happened to him?

I mean with all of the clown's threats I can't be sure. Is he just afraid to talk to me?

Entry 42: Worry

Well it's been a week and nothing has happened. I guess that's a good sign. I'm still not sure what to think about everything. Elliot goes home tomorrow, we've been spending a lot of time together in the past week. He promised me that he would find me once we were both out of the hospital.

But what if things are too different between us? I've thought about this before, but not that much because it wasn't a reality. Now this is happening. I know he promised me that he would find me and we would stay together. But there is still a possibility that we only work while in the hospital. I can't imagine being without him. I don't know if I'm ready to let him go. Things are moving faster than I expected. Elliot was the first real person that I let in after everything that happened. I don't want things to change.

Entry 43: Thinking

So Elliot is gone and I leave tomorrow. I'm so nervous I haven't been able to sleep at all and I've barely eaten. I've tried to keep my nerves in enough so that they didn't think that I had relapsed. Then I would have blown my chances of leaving. I've talked to Jayden some and she already has planned enough things for us to do to last us for years. It has already been decided that I would live with Jayden and her family once I got out. I still haven't heard from Stefan, I hope things are okay, I still worry with all of the new threats.

Although I have thought of another problem. What about school? I hadn't really thought about this until now. I mean I have taken some classes here just to keep up, I was in honors classes before, and so it didn't take much to make sure that I stayed caught up. So I would be going into my senior year of High School. But will I go back to school with Jayden or will I just take classes either online or somewhere else? I guess I should have thought about this sooner. I wonder if Elliot is going back to school as well. But he wouldn't be going to the same school as Jayden and I since he lives in the next district over.

I guess in all of the time I had been here, I never really thought I would get out. I had never thought of a life outside of this hospital ward. I never considered what I would do or who I would be. After I was admitted I never thought of a life outside, back in the real world. For some reason I did not think it was a possibility. Well this is my last lights out. Wish me luck for tomorrow and what's to come.

Entry 44: First Week

So it's been a week since I've been out. I talked to Elliot but only over the phone. He has been busy with a lot of family things and hasn't been able to find the time to come here yet. He is planning to get away this weekend to come and see me. Jayden has been teasing me nonstop about it, but I know she's happy that I finally found some happiness in my life again.

We still have not talked much about what we are going to do after the summer is over. I think that nobody really wants to think about it much. We just want to live in this good moment for once. For once we do not have to worry about the past or the future. We all finally get to live in the moment.

Although a part of me is still worried. It seems like

this is almost too good to be true. That since things are so good right now, that they are bound to come crashing down soon. That something absolutely terrible is just right around the corner.

Although if Jayden heard me talking like this she would tell that I am a worry wart and need to take a chill pill. She would keep cracking jokes until I broke and gave up, abandoning all of those thoughts. I guess I am being paranoid, I do have a tendency to worry too much.

Entry 45: Peace and Goodbyes

So I really was worrying for nothing. Thing are good with everything and everyone. I think I was just being paranoid. Everything seems to have fallen into place. I'm mostly happy for once. I still get the dreams and flashes sometimes, but I'm dealing better than I was before. I still go to therapy but only once every other week now. Miss Taylor said that she was very proud of me and how far I've come. Things are finally looking up for me. This is the beginning of a new chapter in my life.

Although my parents are no longer here to be with me, I know that they would be happy that things are getting better. I am always going to miss them, but I am starting to come to terms with what happened. I am in the process of forgiving myself and realizing that their death was not my fault, that I had no control over what happened that night.

This may be one of the last entries I write. I know you will miss me and my problems (not really). I only started to write this journal because of the hospital and it is what Miss Taylor wanted me to do. But now that I am out of the hospital, I do not think that I need to keep writing. Things are going good and it can be boring to only read and write about good things. People tend to read about the bad things because we always want a happy ending. This might just be it, the happy ending. The bad things have been worked out and now there is nothing left to fix. I don't think I have anything to keep you here anymore. So unless something totally tragic occurs and there will be more entries after this. Not that I want that.

This is goodbye for now. I don't think there is anything more for me to tell you. It was fun while it lasted.

Entry 46: Forget It

This is defiantly not goodbye, I was wrong. So I have had quite the 2 weeks. I've been hanging out with Elliot and Jayden and even Stefan for a bit. He came back from an emergency business trip and forgot his phone and laptop here so that's why he never contacted me back.

But something has been bothering me. Elliot has been acting really weird, and I'm not sure why. When I tried to talk to him about it, he just said that he was sleepy and not to worry about it. I could tell he was lying to me, I just don't know why. I don't know, I hope everything is okay between us.

I was hoping that my fears about our relationship outside of the hospital would not come true. I guess I just can't catch a break.

....

So Elliot is officially avoiding me. When I tried to get a hold of him, his mom answered and said that he can't talk right now and he'll let me know when he is available. That was 4 days ago. Even Jayden tried to get ahold of him and he won't talk to her either. He answered but said he just can't talk right now and to leave him alone. Was it something that I did? Did I do something to upset him? Is this all my fault?

Entry 47: Hurt

I don't know what to think anymore. I feel so betrayed. I trusted Elliot and he completely betrayed me. I can't believe that the first person that I trusted outside of the people that were involved in what happened did something like this to me. I just can't deal with everything that is going on right now.

Entry 48: Story Time

Now that I have calmed down enough to write legibly, I am going to tell you a story.

Once upon a time there was girl. This girl had a great life until tragedy struck and something terrible happened to her and her family. This something scarred the girl so much that she had to go away for a whole year. When she finally began to feel better, she opened her heart.

The girl opened her heart to this boy she met. This boy was also broken too. They were broken together and understood each other like no one else did. They helped to put their broken pieces back together and trusted the other with everything.

Eventually the boy and the girl got to go home. But then things got complicated. Their happiness only lasted about a month once they got back. Until the girl found out that the boy was hiding something.

When the girl found out his secret, she was heartbroken. She had found out that the boy was a part of the terrible thing that had happened to her. He said he did not know at the time. He said he never meant to be a part of it. He said that he did not mean to keep it from her just that he did not know that he was a part of her past until it was too late.

The girl is now even more broken than before. The one person that had helped her start to put her pieces back together was a part of what broke her in the first place.

THE END

So that is my story, sorry there is no happy ending, those do not exist anymore. Just in case you have not put everything together, Elliot played a part in clown incident. The clowns were some of Elliot's friends that had already graduated. Elliot had gotten into the wrong crowd while in school. Elliot was actually the one who picked my house. The clowns had told him that he needed to pick a house and be the getaway car for their raid. If he did not go along with it then they would not let him leave the group like he wanted to. But then things got out hand. People were not supposed to die.

Then Elliot met me and he did not realize the connection until later. It was not until the clowns contacted him again and he refused. That was when they told him about me and that it was his girlfriend's house he picked for the raid.

I do not know what to think. I do not know if I can

forgive Elliot either. I know it is not completely his fault, but he still played a role in it. I cannot just forget something like that. He was first person I let it and now everything is falling apart I do not have anything to hold me together anymore. I mean sure there is Jayden but it is just different. I know she is here for me but it is still not the same as what I had with Elliot.

Elliot and I had a deep connection. We had both been through so much. We were both broken souls and we worked together to put each other's broken pieces together. Now I do not know what to do anymore. He was my glue and my rock. Of course we were not together that long but we made a deep connection within the time we together.

What if I can never trust anyone again? What if this is what pushes me over the edge? Elliot was my last shred of hope and now I've lost it forever. I cannot forget this. Maybe in time I can forgive him but things are just too broken now to fix. There is no going back.

Elliot said he is going to turn himself and the others in. Although I am still deeply hurt by him, I worry for him. What if he gets sent to jail? Would he survive it? What if he was with the others? They surely would not be happy with him for turning them all in. They have already murdered two people that I know.

This is it. This is the bad thing I was worried about. This is the disruption in the peace that was inevitable. This is the turning point in all of our lives. What will happen now?

Entry 49: Anger

It is all over the news, again. Elliot went to the police this morning and confessed. The clowns were also arrested but they tried to deny everything. Stefan and I were called in to try and identify them. We just got back a little bit ago. I did not think I was going to be able to do it. I thought it would all be too much. Stefan went first to give me some breathing room and prepare myself mentally.

It was more difficult than I thought it would be. I had to keep reminding myself that they could not see me through the glass. It has also been well over a year. I was not sure if I could do it. But I knew right away who it was. Even though I had never seen their faces, I knew. I recognized Scar and Burn easily because of their markings. But then Red was bit harder to identify, since none of them had on a red sweatshirt, not that I had expected that.

There was something in his face and his eyes. It was like he knew I was standing on the other side. It was like he was staring straight into my soul. Even though I had never seen his face and he did not have a scar or burn. I knew. I knew it had to be him. No one else would look that smug. He thought he was still going to get away with it. He thought he was in the clear, this was just a game to him.

I will not let him get away this time. I have never felt such anger and determination before. The clowns will not get out of this. I'll show Red who is the master of this game and it is not him. I will win, whatever it takes. Nothing can stop me now.

Entry 50: This Long?

Wow, we have been together for 50 entries now. I feel kind of proud that we made it this far. We have been through a lot in the last 49 entries. But unfortunately I think that we still have a lot left to go through before we reach an end to this story.

I am still unsure how I feel about the whole Elliot situation. I still love him, but we are too poisonous for each other. He would only remind me of what happened and I would only remind him of his guilt and what he was a part of. I think that it is for the best if we just go our separate ways. I will treasure the short but sweet time that we did share. I won't associate the good memories with the terrible end it all came to. I'd rather keep them separate from each other.

This is not a goodbye just a see you later for now. There are still some things that need working out.

Entry 51: Solutions

I know it has been awhile but I am back. The trails are over now. All of the clowns and Elliot were found guilty. They won't be getting out any time soon. The only one that would is Elliot. Also I found out that Elliot is going to a different prison than the clowns, which makes me feel relieved. Even after his betrayal, I still worry and care for him.

I might decide to go and visit him sometime but I am not sure. Things are still tense between us, I know he feels extremely guilty for everything. He even turned himself and the others in after he confessed to me. He didn't have to do that. I understand that and I truly do believe that I will be able to forgive him. Maybe not now or soon, but eventually.

Although I don't know if I can find true happiness again. I know I still have Stefan and Jayden but I don't know if I can trust anyone else outside of my circle again. I know that nobody else could be a part of what happened but now I feel like I am always going to set myself up to be crushed and betrayed. Not to mention that I would have to find someone that could handle all of my baggage and there is a lot of it.

Entry 52: Memory Cage

I have memories that I cannot escape. They taunt me in my dreams and in the shadows of day. I have episodes where I can't focus on anything else. It consumes me until it's hard to breathe. I become completely unresponsive to anyone and anything. They trap me in their cage and throw away the key. I can't get out without help.

Jayden has helped me through these kind of episodes a lot. I tend to hide in a corner or the bathroom when they come like this. If I'm not already in the bathroom, Jayden has to get me there and in the bathtub. The only way to get me out is to put me under the shower head with slightly cold water. It is the only thing that can break me out of my memory cage. It shocks my system enough to break my trance.

I don't think the episodes will ever stop. They may become less often, but they will always be there no matter what. I will always be running from my memory cage that refuses to leave me. Why did this happen now, on my 18th birthday? Of all the days, it had to be today.

Entry 53: Reaching Out

So it's been awhile, about a year now since my last entry. I have come to better terms with everything that happened. I've even written a letter to Elliot. I'll leave a copy here for you.

Dear Elliot,

I know it's been a long time since we last spoke and we ended on some bad terms. We've been through a lot together and we opened up to each other about our darkest secrets and troubled pasts. I miss what we once had, we had a good run while it lasted. Maybe some things just weren't meant to last but they were an experience that you needed.

I just wanted to let you know that I forgive you. I understand that you didn't mean for everything to happen the way it did. They had forced you do it and you couldn't have known what would have been the result or that you would meet me. You also didn't have to tell me. You could've kept your involvement a secret, but you didn't. So thank you for that.

I'm so grateful for everything that you did for me. There is no need for you to feel guilty anymore. It wasn't your fault. Everything is okay with us and I mean it. **I forgive you.** I hope that one day we can be friends again, I'd like that. I still care for you and you played big role in my life. Thank you for everything, it means a lot.

Sincerely,
Violet L. Andrews

So that is my letter. I hope he reads it and he believes me. I truly do forgive him for what happened, he didn't have a choice and I can't blame him for that. It's the clowns that are responsible. It will still be a long, long time before I forgive them, if I ever do. All there is left to do now is wait.

Entry 54: Response

Elliot has written me back. He explained how sorry he was and how thankful he was for my forgiveness. He told me that he may be up for parole in a year or so. I think I'm going to testify to make sure he gets it or something that would help. I worry about him being in jail. I hope he is okay.

I'm glad that we are on better terms now. It feels like a weight has been lifted off of my shoulders. I've finally found some peace for once. Although for some reason I don't think this is quite goodbye yet. I think there is still a little bit more that needs happen. Until then.

Entry 55: Anniversary

Today is the 2 year anniversary of my parents' death and the official death of my childhood. I feel better than I had expected. It hurts but not as bad as it once did. It doesn't paralyze me anymore. I still breathe, although there are moments when it gets hard and I have to take a moment to focus on getting my lungs to operate properly again. I have an amazing support system though. I think I can make it out of this alive. Eventually someday I will be okay. I will always miss my parents and what I once had. What could have been today is things hadn't changed like they did.

I visited them today at the cemetery. I bought some nice flowers and replaced the old and withered ones that were there. Seeing them there made it more real for some reason, even after all of this time. They really are gone. But at least now they are in a better place and they are happy. There is no more pain for them. I'm glad they've found their peace.

Entry 56: New Beginnings

So quite a bit has happened in the last few weeks. Stefan came back home and now we are living together in an apartment for now until I graduate and move out. I've gone back to school with Jayden and reconnected with some old friends. Although I've lost some along the way, I'm happy with those who stayed and accepted me for who I am. I still see Miss Taylor, just not as often. We've become somewhat of friends through all of this.

I have also met someone new. He goes to my school and his name is Kai. He is full of light and happiness. He may not have baggage like Elliot and I had, but he helps me to edge away my darkness. Kai accepts me for who I am and his light balances out my dark. My past does not bother him even though I haven't shared all of it with it him. He embraces it and is so good to me. He does not rush me in anything and he knows about Elliot. I can't believe that I found happiness again, I guess I was wrong.

Entry 57: Goodbye

So it's been just over a year now. Elliot got parole and we are good friends. Kai and I are still together and we are very happy, although I haven't told him about the terrible thing yet, I think I'll tell him soon though. I trust him enough. Kai and Elliot are also friends, they understand each other. Elliot is happy for me, he knows how much Kai helps and means to me. Elliot has also found someone that makes him happy and helps him in the way that Kai helps me. Her name is Ivy. We've actually become pretty good friends. Jayden and I both graduated High School and started collage this past fall.

Well I guess this is it. There is nothing left for me to write about. This is the end, this is it. I guess this is goodbye now, for good this time. I still don't know you are, but I hope that you had fun on this journey with me. This is harder than I thought it would be. I feel like we have become somewhat of friends now, even though I know absolutely nothing about you, not even your name. You know pretty much everything about me. I guess that's the beauty in it though isn't it? Well wish me luck. I'm off to bigger and better things now. Goodbye my mysterious reader friend.

Entry 58: Thank You

Dear Violet,

Thank you for everything. I understand you even better now. I'm glad that you trusted me enough to read this. By the time you read my letter I would've already done what I'm planning. I picked out the ring and planned the perfect the night, all before you gave me this. I still plan to go through with it, even after this. I love you for who you are, this does not change that and I do not care how much baggage you have. I'm going to propose to you tomorrow and then give you this back. I hope you say yes, Otherwise this will be extremely awkward.

With love,

Kai

Entry 59: Yes

Of course I said yes. I can't believe I am going to get married! I guess my baggage wasn't as heavy as I thought when I have someone that can help me carry it. I really am on to bigger and better things.

Entry 60: The End

So I've been married for about 2 and a half years now. I just had my first child. It was a girl and we named her Clara after my mom. I have found my peace. I still miss my parents but the hurt is not as bad. I no longer ache for hours on end. The pain of the past has lessened and things are much better now. I've also gotten a part time job working as a writer for my college's newspaper. Things are really looking up for me now.

I still keep in contact with Stefan. He is back in Europe and engaged to his girlfriend Amber. They are happy together and I like Amber, she is really sweet and good for Stefan. Jayden has been dating someone for about 7 months now and she's happy. Everyone seems to be doing well. Things are at peace and there are no major troubles anymore. Okay, this is really goodbye now, I promise. Thanks for being here through everything. Wish me luck.

About the Author

By: Jessica Morton

The author, December Weestrand, born and raised in Illinois; wrote the book My Baggage after one of her best friends inspired her. She loves bowling and she's been doing it for almost her whole life. She loves hanging out with family and friends. December is an avid reader. She loves to tell a good story. Her passion for literature has compelled her to this, her first novel entitled 'My Baggage'.

"The most important thing is to enjoy your life - to be happy - it's all that matters."

Audrey Hepburn

Lightning Source UK Ltd.
Milton Keynes UK
UKHW020154160119
335557UK00002B/56/P